Roger goes Back to the Desert

Written by: Manmeet Narang

Edited by: Tapasi De, Monika Tyagi and Akanksha Arora

Illustrated by: Suman S. Roy

Roger the camel lived in a park. The park was in a city near a desert. Every evening, children came to the park to play. They loved to ride on his back. Roger liked to see children but he wanted to go back to the desert.

One day Roger was sitting under the shade of the tree. He heard a humming sound. He looked up. A tiny bird with blue and grey feathers was sitting on the tree.

'Hey! My name is Roger. You sing very well,' said Roger. 'Hi. I am Debbie. I am not singing. When I flutter my wings, there is a humming sound,' explained Debbie.

'You flutter your wings so fast?' Roger said. 'Yes, that is why my wings make the humming sound,' said Debbie. She flew down and sat on the flowers.

'Are you smelling the beautiful flowers?' asked Roger. 'I cannot smell anything. I am sucking nectar. I like nectar of the flowers but sometimes I also eat insects,' explained Debbie.

Just then, David came. He gave some grass to Roger. David had brought Roger from the desert and took care of him. Roger started eating the grass.

'But I only eat plants and grass. With my thick lips, I can also eat thorns. If I am really hungry, I can even eat shoes. Ha! Ha! Ha!' Roger laughed.

Roger drank all the water lying in the tub. Debbie was surprised to see him drink so much of water in one go. Roger smiled, 'I can also swim Debbie!' Debbie was impressed.

Debbie flew up in the sky. She turned left, then right. Then she flew up and down. She sat on the flowers and sucked the nectar again. 'Wow Debbie! You can fly in all directions. Wait I will also show you something,' Roger said.

He tried to get up. It took him some time to lift his body. Then he began to kick with all his four legs. First left and then right. 'Wow Roger! You can kick with all your four legs, just the way I can fly in all directions,' Debbie clapped.

Debbie saw an insect on the ground. She picked it up in her beak and gobbled it. 'You are a tiny bird but you eat a lot!' Roger smiled. 'I flutter my wings so much that I get tired. I need food every few minutes to get energy,' explained Debbie.

'I am also feeling tired,' Roger yawned and went to sleep. Debbie sat in a corner of the tree. 'Wake up you lazy fellow!' David shouted. Roger did not move.

'It is so difficult to wake you up. Get up!' David shook Roger. Roger yawned. Debbie laughed, 'I thought I was the only one who took a long time to get up. But you are just like me.'

Roger sat up. It was evening. The park was full of children. There was a long queue of children waiting for Roger to give them a ride.

David was happy. He had earned good money that day. But Roger was sad and tired. David gave him some more grass to eat.

'Why are you so sad Roger?' Debbie asked. 'My feet and my back are paining,' said Roger. He looked with sad eyes at Debbie.

'Why don't you go back to the desert?' asked Debbie. 'David will never let me go. He earns money from the rides. He keeps me tied with this rope all the time,' said Roger.

Debbie began to think. She made a plan. 'Roger let's trouble David so much that he will set you free,' Debbie was smiling at her clever plan. Roger listened to the plan with excitement.

At night, Roger began to moan and groan. David got up from his sleep. 'Don't make noise!' David scolded Roger. After sometime, Roger again began to make noise.

David was very irritated. 'I will tie you far away now,' David said angrily. The moment he opened the rope, Roger kicked him hard with his leg.

David fell on the ground. Roger picked up his shoes and began to eat. 'My shoes! This camel has gone mad,' David cried.

Roger marched towards him. Now David was really scared. He ran away crying 'Help! Help!' The plan had worked. Both Debbie and Roger laughed.

Roger ran outside the gate of the park. Debbie flew and sat on his back. 'It is fun to take a ride on your back Roger. Will you take me along with you to the desert?' asked Debbie.

'How will you eat nectar little bird? There are no flowers in the desert. There are no trees where you can sleep,' said Roger.

'Oh my God! How do you live there Roger?' 'I can live for days without food. Do you see that hump on my back? My food stays stored there,' Roger explained.

'I think I am happy here. You have fun in the desert,' Debbie said. 'Thank you for helping me Debbie. I will miss your songs,' Roger said, sadly.

'But who will wake you up in the desert?' asked Debbie. 'No one. I will wake up when I want to. I am free now!' Roger smiled.

Vocabulary

humming
flutter
explained
sucking
explained
surprised
impressed
sucked
nectar

gobbled
yawned
lazy
queue
excitement
moan
groan
marched
scared

Fact File

Camel

- Camels can kick with all the four legs.
- Due to their thick lips, they can eat thorny plants also. They can also eat shoes if hungry!
- Camels moan and groan.
- The hump stores their food and they can stay without food for days.
- Camels can drink large quantity of water in one go.
- Camels can swim.
- Camels take time to get up. Once they sleep, it is difficult to wake them up.

Hummingbird

- Hummingbird is the smallest bird.
- When it flutters its wings, there is a humming sound.
- It flutters its wings very fast, that is why it needs food after a few minutes.
- It doesn't have a sense of smell.
- It eats nectar from flowers and insects.
- It flies in all directions.
- It takes a long time to get up from sleep.

Activity

Learn from the story

Help your child comprehend the story and develop an understanding of values of life through the experiences of the characters. Ask them questions and encourage them to think, ponder and seek answers. This will trigger their critical thinking, creativity and curiosity.

1. Why did Roger not like to be in the city?
2. Do you think David was a good caretaker?
3. Why can't Debbie and Roger live together in the desert?
4. What kind of bird was Debbie? Brave or weak?
5. A camel is called the 'ship of the desert'. Why do you think he is called by that name?